MY MOMMY

I Got Adopted!

written by
Lauren Barrett

TATE PUBLISHING
& Enterprises

This title is also available as a Tate Out Loud product. Visit www.tatepublishing.com for more information.

The opinions expressed by the author are not necessarily those of Tate Publishing, LLC.

Published by Tate Publishing & Enterprises, LLC
127 E. Trade Center Terrace | Mustang, Oklahoma 73064 USA
1.888.361.9473 | www.tatepublishing.com

Tate Publishing is committed to excellence in the publishing industry. The company reflects the philosophy established by the founders, based on Psalm 68:11,
"The Lord gave the word and great was the company of those who published it."

Book design copyright © 2009 by Tate Publishing, LLC. All rights reserved.
Cover and Interior design by Elizabeth A. Mason
Illustrations by Greg White

Published in the United States of America

ISBN: 978-1-60799-407-7
1. Juvenile Fiction: Family: Adoption
2. Juvenile Fiction: Social Issues: New Experiences
09.05.13

Without the support of my parents, my sister, Debi, who traveled to China with me, and the support of my cousin DarLea, who offered ongoing encouragement, this story might not have reached publication. I would like to thank them all. A very special thank you to my parents, who made it all possible. Last but not least, a thank you to my beautiful daughter, Hayley, who has enriched my life and our family.

The rain splashed against the windows and woke me up early one morning; then I heard people saying my name over and over and then giggling at the news. I, Han Fumei, was going to America!

What's that? I wondered and grabbed my soft yellow blanket. Some of the nannies were crying when they came to my crib and hugged me tightly, so I started to cry too. I was scared. I didn't know what was happening.

My favorite nanny had long hair that she put in a ponytail. She touched my cheek softly while she told me, "Han Fumei, you are a very special baby. A woman from a faraway country is coming to China to adopt one of our babies, and you have been chosen for this honor. You will be going to live with her and have a wonderful life with everything that we can't give you here."

I didn't want to live with a stranger, but my nanny wanted me to go. Her cheek was warm on my face as she held me, and I felt her crying on my jammies.

One day, the nannies decided that I needed a nice warm bath. Squirming and kicking did not get me out of it; they just laughed and put me in the water!

"Fumei, sit still," one of them said. It was slippery in that old white sink, but I slapped and played with the pretty bubbles as a nanny held me up so I didn't fall over. I did not like it when they washed my hair, and I fussed and cried. My nanny rinsed me and dried me with a big towel, but then I got the shivers.

Later, I felt like it was Chinese New Year after I was dressed. I wore lots of clothes under my gold-colored outfit. "You won't be cold, Han Fumei," one nanny said. "See how big and chubby you look, too." She laughed and tickled me under my chin.

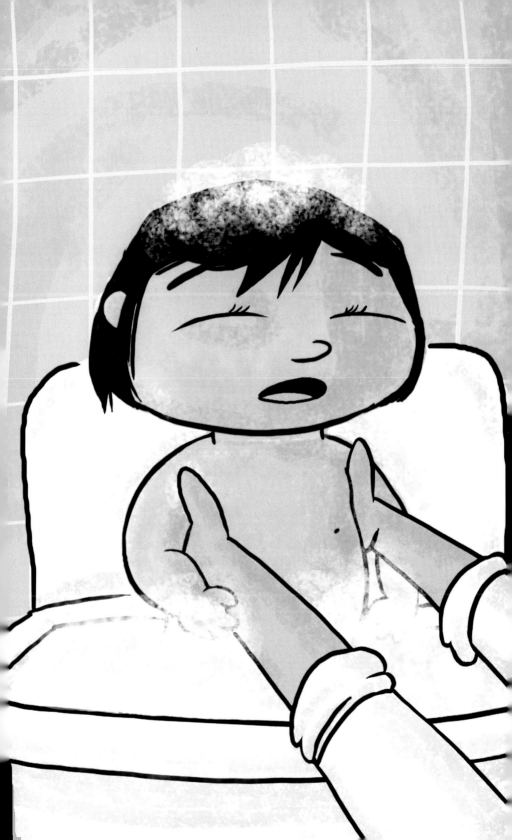

I was stiff with all those clothes and hot, but I loved my beautiful red and black silk slippers. When I wiggled my toes, I could make the tassels jiggle all over. *Where are we going?* I wondered.

Bright lights shined on me as I stood on a wobbly white chair for something called a photograph. I held a round, shiny bracelet for the picture. This was to be the first picture of me that my new mommy would see.

While I waited for new mommy to come for me, I played in my tiny crib. I liked to look at the cracks in the ceiling and pretend they were animals, but I heard and saw other babies like me in their cribs. Were they waiting for mommies too?

One day, my nanny gave me a bottle of milk and said, "Han Fumei, it's time. Your new mommy is in China. I must take you to her."

She dressed me in my sleeper with little red elephants on it and my green plastic shoes. A man with a pigtail and hair growing under his nose took us to the city in a blue car. Shaking, I leaned against my nanny, worrying about leaving the babies' room. Nanny held me up, and I saw grass, tall trees, and red flowers called roses. I felt afraid and didn't want to leave.

"Say good-bye," my nanny whispered. I turned in her lap and looked at the building that was my home get smaller as we drove away. I cried and snuggled in closer to my nanny.

"We're here," called the driver. I felt really scared as we went into a tan building with colored flags flying in front. We stood outside a room full of people. *Who are they?*

"Next!" someone said. My name was called and another that sounded strange. *What is going on?*

"Soon, my pretty, soon," said my nanny. She stood up slowly and carried me into that room full of people. I could feel her heart beating behind the buttons on her blouse.

Was she afraid too? I wanted to go home.

But there, standing in the middle of a group of black-haired men, was the strangest lady I've ever seen. I gasped. *This can't be my new mommy!*

"There she is, Fumei," my favorite nanny whispered. She squeezed me tighter.

That tall, smiling lady had pale skin, blue colored eyes, and the funniest hair, all curly and yellow. She reached out her arms for me, and, of course, I screamed and clung to my nanny, but I was handed over to the new mommy anyway.

She held me gently and touched my hair softly. "Hello, Han Fumei." *Han Fumei?* How did she know my name? She smiled at me. "Don't be afraid; I won't hurt you." I didn't know her words, and her voice was nice, but I cried and cried until I fell asleep in her lap.

My nanny was gone when I woke up. I stared up at my new mommy, and she looked back at me with love in her eyes and hugged me. We rode in a bus to a fancy hotel, and she sat me up so that I could see outside. This time I saw lots of people riding bicycles. Finally, I just couldn't stand it any longer. I reached up to touch that fluffy, yellow hair. It felt soft!

My new mommy seemed very happy, but the lady who was with her just kept crying and crying. *Why are you crying?* I tried to ask her, but she didn't answer me. She just smiled at me and touched my cheek.

As I started to feel better, I snuggled against this new mommy person, and I felt safe. "I love you very much, Han Fumei," she said to me. My nanny told me that this new mommy would love me and take care of me always and give me a forever family. I smiled at Mommy. She kissed me... I wasn't afraid anymore.

e|LIVE

listen|imagine|view|experience

AUDIO BOOK DOWNLOAD INCLUDED WITH THIS BOOK!

In your hands you hold a complete digital entertainment package. Besides purchasing the paper version of this book, this book includes a free download of the audio version of this book. Simply use the code listed below when visiting our website. Once down-loaded to your computer, you can listen to the book through your computer's speakers, burn it to an audio CD or save the file to your portable music device (such as Apple's popular iPod) and listen on the go!

How to get your free audio book digital download:

1. Visit www.tatepublishing.com and click on the e|LIVE logo on the home page.
2. Enter the following coupon code:
   7ca0-11b5-c579-1784-b05c-356f-5fa3-0204
3. Download the audio book from your e|LIVE digital locker and begin enjoying your new digital entertainment package today!